NORTHBROOK PUBLIC LIBRARY
1201 CE
NORTHBRC

W9-DES-011

2018

Northbrook Public Library

3 1123 01196 6374

DISNEY
PRINCESS
BEGINNINGS

TIANA'S
Best Surprise

BY TESSA ROEHL

ILLUSTRATED BY
THE DISNEY STORYBOOK ART TEAM

Random House New York

For Nels

—T. R.

Copyright © 2018 Disney Enterprises, Inc. All rights reserved. Published in the United States by Random House Children's Books, a division of Penguin Random House LLC, 1745 Broadway, New York, NY 10019, and in Canada by Penguin Random House Canada Limited, Toronto, in conjunction with Disney Enterprises, Inc. Random House and the colophon are registered trademarks of Penguin Random House LLC.

rhcbooks.com

Library of Congress Cataloging-in-Publication Data is available upon request.
ISBN 978-0-7364-3759-2 (trade) — ISBN 978-0-7364-9021-4 (lib. bdg.)

Printed in the United States of America
10 9 8 7 6 5 4 3 2 1

Book design by Jenna Huerta & Betty Avila

This book has been officially leveled by using the F&P Text Level Gradient™ Leveling System.

Random House Children's Books supports the First Amendment and celebrates the right to read.

Chapter 1
A Delicious Dream

Tiana's eyes opened wide. It had only been a dream. But it felt so real, she could still smell it: the spices, the bubbling broth, and all the love stirred into the gumbo. She could see it, too: Happy faces sharing the meal, her daddy happiest of all. Enjoying gumbo so perfect it sparkled. The *best* gumbo ever.

It was early. Earlier than the time her mama usually popped her head in and said,

"Tiana, up and at 'em. The stars have gone to bed, and it's your turn to shine now." The sun was just starting to peek through her window. But it wasn't the morning light that had woken her. It was her dream and the plan that had started forming in her head.

Tiana threw off her covers, got dressed, made her bed, and darted out of her room. There wasn't a drop of sleep left in her now.

She burst into the kitchen, ready to tell her mama all about the dream and the plan. But the sight of her daddy at the stove closed her mouth up tight before the words could tumble out. She ran to his side, wrapping her arms around his waist.

He smiled down at her, that smile where his mouth stretched wide and his eyes crinkled, making her feel as warm as the heat rising from the stove. Tiana almost never got the chance to see him off to work. He left too early, when the sky was still dark. "Perfect timing," he said. "I'm making the *best* scrambled eggs ever."

"The best?" Tiana asked.

"That's what he keeps saying." Tiana's mama laughed. She was seated at the kitchen table.

"Well," her daddy said, frowning, "they *will* be the best scrambled eggs ever . . . once Tiana tells me what they're missing."

Tiana grinned. She took the bite he was holding out for her to taste.

"Now, don't you say hot sauce, because that's already in there," he said.

"I *know*, Daddy. I can taste it," Tiana said. "Hmmm." She closed her eyes, focusing on the flavors on her tongue. Salt, pepper, onion, parsley . . . *Aha!* "Bell peppers!" she cried.

"Bell peppers, you say?" Her daddy reached into the vegetable bin.

Tiana nodded. "They'll add just the right crunch."

He handed Tiana a red bell pepper and watched her make careful cuts. "Eudora,

I've taught this girl well in her eight years, haven't I?"

"You sure have, James," her mama said. "Taught her nose to wake her up for a good breakfast. Is that what got you rushing down here so early, Tiana?"

Tiana avoided looking at her mother and focused on scooping the peppers into the eggs. Her daddy handed her the spoon to continue stirring as he fetched plates from the cupboard. The dream she'd had about *the best gumbo ever* was still right there in her head. But she couldn't say anything about it yet. Part of what was going to make it the best ever was that it would be a surprise. "I've got to start waking up early, Mama. Practice for our restaurant."

"Tiana's Place," her daddy said, winking at her as he took the spoon back and served up the eggs.

"Tiana's Place," Tiana agreed, helping him carry the plates to the table.

"Tiana's Place," her mama chimed in as she began eating. "Once New Orleans gets a taste of your daddy's gumbo, folks will be lining up for blocks. You'll have to wake up well before the sun to prepare for all those customers."

Tiana blew on her eggs to cool them down. "I won't sleep ever again if it means

Daddy and I can have our restaurant." Her daddy had been working so much lately, she barely got to see him anymore. She knew it was good for their savings, which her daddy kept in coffee cans that he stuffed with his extra bills and coins. The cans were getting fuller and fuller. Someday soon, they'd be able to afford Tiana's Place. But she wanted him to take a break and have someone do something nice for him for once. That was where her plan came in.

Her daddy stood up, his plate empty. Her mama held out his lunch pail. "Hard work is going to get us that restaurant, and that's what I'm off to do." He kissed Tiana on the top of her head. "Sleep is pretty important, too, though. Two more days and then it's Sunday and I'll have the whole evening free." He looked over his shoulder as he opened the door. "Maybe we can make something for dinner? What do you say, Tiana?"

"No!" Tiana nearly spit out her eggs as she yelled. Her father looked confused. "I mean . . . Sunday's your birthday. You shouldn't have to work on your birthday," she finished, shooting a glance at her mother for help.

Her mama laughed. "We've got your birthday plans covered." Her daddy ruffled Tiana's hair, and then he was gone.

Tiana's mother gave her a knowing look. "What's cooking in that head of yours?"

"Mama, I had the most delicious dream." Tiana set her fork down and pushed her plate away.

"Delicious?" her mama asked. She pointed back at Tiana's plate, her eyes telling Tiana she'd better eat up.

Tiana took two more bites. "I saw it, Mama. In my dream. *I* made the *best* gumbo ever."

"You and your daddy already make the

best gumbo ever. Everyone on this block knows so." Her mama pointed at the plate again.

"But this time I made it all by myself. No help from Daddy—just his gumbo pot, of course." Tiana took another bite before her mama could give her that look again. "It was so perfect, it sparkled! And everyone from the neighborhood was there to taste it, and . . . oh, Mama, best of all: we surprised Daddy! I've never seen him so happy."

"That is a lovely dream, baby."

Tiana swallowed the last bite and took

the breakfast plates to the sink to wash. "I'm going to make it real," she said. "Since Sunday is Daddy's birthday, we'll invite everyone over for a party, only he won't know about it. And he won't know I've already made the gumbo. All he'll have to do is show up! It'll be perfect."

Her mama joined her at the sink to help dry the dishes. "I agree. If you're in charge, it will be perfect."

Tiana smiled. "Oh, and Big Daddy and Charlotte will come, of course."

"Of course." Her mama nodded. "Seeing as how Sunday is the day after tomorrow, I think we'd better go tell the neighbors your plan, don't you?"

"Yes!" Tiana was thrilled. Her dream was going to come true.

Chapter 2
The New Neighbor

An hour later, when the neighborhood began to stir, Tiana and her mama set out to visit their neighbors before everyone left for school, work, or errands. Tiana skipped off the porch and grabbed her mom's hand, tugging her across the street to the Johnsons' house. Marnie Johnson, who everyone called Grandma Marnie, was already outside in her rocking chair.

"Good morning, Tiana, dear. Morning, Eudora."

"Grandma Marnie!" Tiana called. Her mama squeezed her hand. "Oh, I mean, good morning," she said. "We're having a party for my daddy on Sunday. At five p.m. It's a surprise!"

Grandma Marnie nodded, still rocking away. "You know I'll be there. Gumbo?"

"Gumbo," Tiana said. "I'm going to make it all by myself."

"If it's half as good as your daddy's, be sure you make extra."

Her mother waved good-bye. "Give my best to the family, Marnie."

"And tell all the Johnsons to come," Tiana added.

"Oh, but if they come, that's less gumbo for me." Grandma Marnie chuckled.

Tiana continued to the house next door, her mama close behind. Little Emile Monroe opened the door just a crack, peeking out at Tiana, his eyes wide. He quickly slammed it shut.

"Sugar, can you go fetch your mama for us?" Tiana's

mother called through the door. Footsteps sounded from inside.

"Why is he so afraid of me and not of you? I'm closer to his age!" Tiana exclaimed. She never understood why Emile always hid from her.

Her mama laughed. "Sometimes a little sugar goes farther than spice, Tiana."

Tiana shook her head. That didn't make any sense.

Moments later, Emile's mama, Annette Monroe, came to the door.

"Look at you two, out and about so early." Annette grinned. Tiana had always liked Annette. Something in her eyes made Tiana feel as if she knew how to have fun. As if she would definitely throw a fantastic surprise party.

"Tiana has something she'd like to ask you," her mom said.

"We're having a surprise party for my daddy on Sunday evening. I'll be making gumbo, and all the Monroes are expected to be there," Tiana said.

"Are we, now?" Annette laughed. Emile was peeking out from behind her. Tiana frowned at him, and he darted back behind his mother's skirt. "Well, in that case, we'll be there. Your dad is lucky to have such a thoughtful daughter."

Tiana hopped off the porch. "See you Sunday! Five o'clock! Bye, Emile!" As she waved, Emile ran out of sight.

Tiana and her mom continued down the block. They stopped at the Dupres', the Potters', the Keans', the Gilmores', the Rices', and finally, the Wildes'. After Mr. Wilde quizzed Tiana on her gumbo recipe and she answered his questions to his satisfaction, she was ready to go home and get planning. She started to head back, when her mom stopped her.

"Tiana, we haven't reached the end of the block," her mama said.

"We've called on everyone, Mama."

"Not everyone." Her mama pointed at the next house, the last one on the street. Tiana had never visited the house before. As far as she knew, no one lived there. The houses on her block weren't grand. They were nothing like the houses where Big Daddy and Charlotte lived. They were smaller, not filled with fancy furniture, elegant drapes, or shiny silver. They were stuffed tight with family, food, and a few possessions. And, of course, love. But the house her mama was pointing at looked older and smaller than

the others on the block. Was the inside going to be like the rest of the houses she knew? Or would it be different?

Her mama took her by the hand again. "Nothing to worry about, Tiana. Just someone new for you to meet."

"Someone new?" Tiana wasn't sure how to feel about someone new. She hadn't seen any *new* faces in her dream.

"Mrs. Isabel Marquez. She just moved in last month. We should include everyone and welcome her to the neighborhood. That's what your daddy would do, isn't it?" Her mama gazed down at her.

Tiana's daddy always said that what he

loved about food was how it brought people together. All people. Tiana nodded and let her mother lead her toward the house. Besides, she thought, someone new to taste her gumbo—that was surely a good thing. She quickened her pace and even felt a little excited when her mom knocked on the door.

An older woman opened it. She was older than Tiana's mama for sure, though not quite as old as Grandma Marnie. Her gray hair was gathered in a bun. Her face was serious, but her skin looked soft. "Good morning," the woman said. The way she spoke sounded different from the way Tiana and her mama spoke. Tiana had heard lots of different accents around New Orleans: French, Creole, German, Irish, Italian, and more. But she wasn't sure what this accent was.

"Good morning," Tiana said.

"Mrs. Marquez, you may remember me from when I came by just after you moved in. I'm Eudora. This is my daughter, Tiana. She has something to ask you." Tiana's mama squeezed her hand. She was always sending messages with those squeezes.

Tiana gulped, feeling shyer than she

had in a long while and wanting to hide behind her mother's skirts, like Emile. But the gumbo and her daddy's surprise were more important. "We're having a party on Sunday night at five o'clock. For my daddy. It's a surprise. We'd—I'd like you to come. I'm making gumbo."

"Gumbo?" Mrs. Marquez asked.

"Have you tasted New Orleans gumbo yet?" Tiana asked. "I promise you'll like it. No one on earth can taste it and not like it."

Mrs. Marquez smiled. Or at least, Tiana thought it was a smile. She wasn't sure. Something about this woman seemed nervous, too, as if she might want skirts of her own to hide behind. "*Sí*. Yes. Gumbo. I would like that very much." She nodded at Tiana. "Thank you, Tiana. Thank you, Eudora." Mrs. Marquez rolled the *r* in *Eudora*. Tiana liked it. It sounded like . . . yes, that was it — Spanish.

"Looking forward to seeing you then," Tiana's mom said. And with that, Tiana and her mother headed home.

"That wasn't so bad, was it?" her mama asked.

Tiana shook her head. "Not so bad at all. Can we go shopping for ingredients now?"

"Now? It's Friday," her mama said as they walked back inside their house. "You've got to get off to school soon, and I've got a dress to finish up for Charlotte. But tomorrow, when I deliver it, you can come along. We'll stop by the big market in town afterward. Deal?"

A visit to her best friend, and a chance to shop at the big city market? "Deal!" Tiana exclaimed.

Chapter 3
Charlotte's Idea

The next day, Tiana and her mother took the streetcar to Charlotte and Big Daddy's house. As they walked through the garden toward the big double doors of the mansion, a cloud of pink and yellow ran through the neatly trimmed trees. Charlotte was racing toward them, followed by her puppy, Stella, and her cat, Marcel.

"Tiana, Tiana, Tiana!" Charlotte threw

her arms around Tiana, almost knocking her over. Charlotte's big blue eyes were nearly hidden by the blond curls that had fallen into her face. "I didn't know you were coming today!"

Stella yipped, circling everyone's ankles. Marcel hung back, eyeing the action. He had a habit of getting trampled when Charlotte got excited.

"We just planned it yesterday. I have a surprise to tell you about!" Tiana said.

Charlotte clasped her hands to her mouth and squealed. "A surprise? Oh, oh, tell me, tell me!"

But before Tiana could say anything,

her mama took both girls gently by the shoulders and steered them toward the big double doors. "Let's talk surprises as we get this dress fitted."

Charlotte skipped up the front steps to her house. "A surprise *and* a new dress? What a day!"

In Charlotte's room, Tiana sat on the plush carpet under the large window that looked out onto the back gardens. Charlotte was in the middle of the room, covered in lace, ribbon, and taffeta. She was squirming and wriggling as Tiana's mom sewed a delicate row of beads along the dress collar.

"Charlotte, dear. I don't think you would like it much if you bumped into this needle." Tiana's mama was being very patient.

Charlotte clenched her fists and stood still. "If Tiana would just tell me her surprise already, I might be able to calm down."

Stella crawled into Tiana's lap. Tiana responded by giving her a belly rub. "I'm throwing a surprise party for my dad. Tomorrow night. You and Big Daddy are invited!"

Charlotte's eyes grew wide. She jiggled her feet and leapt toward Tiana. Tiana's mama held her in place, clutching the ribbon around her shoulder. Charlotte took a step back. "A surprise party?"

Tiana nodded. "Yes! I was inspired by a dream I had."

"A dream?" Charlotte squealed.

"Yup!" Tiana said. She knew Charlotte would love that part. "And in my dream, I made the *best* gumbo ever. Mama and I are going to the market later to buy all the ingredients."

"Oh, my!" Charlotte was about to burst out of her dress with excitement. "I love a good party. And a good surprise! You must let me help."

"Do you want to come over and help me cook?" Tiana asked.

Charlotte nodded as she scooped Marcel into her arms, running her hands through his white fur. "I want to help you with *everything*! We can go to the market together, we can cook together, we can do it all." Charlotte turned to Tiana's mother. "Miss Eudora, could Big Daddy and I please take Tiana to the market? Then she could stay the night and we could cook the gumbo here."

"Oh, please, Mama," Tiana chimed in. But then a thought struck her. "If I cook here, I won't have my daddy's gumbo pot. . . ."

"We have every kind of pot you could imagine. And besides," Charlotte continued, "if you're cooking in your own kitchen, how will you keep the gumbo a secret from your dad?"

"That's true," Tiana said. She hadn't considered that. Her daddy would know what was happening the minute he got home. "Mama?" Tiana looked up at her mother.

"As long as Big Daddy says it's okay, it's okay with me," her mama said.

"EEEEEE!" Charlotte squealed. Marcel flew out of her arms and ran from the room. Charlotte clasped Tiana's hands and the two friends danced up and down. "This is going to be the greatest surprise party ever!"

Chapter 4
The French Market

Getting Big Daddy to agree to Charlotte and Tiana's plan was as easy as Charlotte saying please. He could never say no to his daughter. So Charlotte changed out of her new dress, Tiana's mama left for home, and the girls headed out the door with Big Daddy for the French Market.

Tiana had been to some of the markets in New Orleans before, but not the French

Market. It was bigger, grander, noisier, and more exciting than anything she had ever seen. Everywhere she looked there was someone shouting, selling, buying, sampling, laughing, bargaining, or arguing. People were bustling back and forth, purchasing the freshest ingredients for their weekend suppers. The air was filled with the scent of fresh seafood, steaming hot bread, strange spices, and sweet sugary somethings. Tiana's eyes were as big as saucers—*this* was where she wanted to be. Maybe one day, she'd come back with her daddy to buy ingredients for Tiana's Place.

Charlotte and Tiana stayed close to Big

Daddy, who, dressed in his finest Saturday suit, was the perfect person to head into a crowd with. Not only was he tall, he was also important. He ran the biggest sugar company in Louisiana, so he was no stranger to the market. Everyone seemed to know who he was and made way for him and the girls.

"Where should we go first, Tiana?" Charlotte asked.

"These are the ingredients I need." Tiana set down her shopping basket and showed Charlotte the recipe she had written out the night before. "What my daddy always uses. His special blend of salt, pepper, cayenne, thyme, and oregano. Flour and butter for the roux—"

"The what? The roo?" Charlotte scrunched her nose.

"Roux. It's French. Fat and flour together. It's the most important part, the base of the whole gumbo!" Tiana continued scanning her recipe. "The holy vegetable trinity: celery, bell peppers, and onions. Sausage and hot sauce, without a doubt, and if I can drive a *hard bargain* like my daddy always does"—Tiana clutched a small coin purse in her hand—"I'll have enough left for crab." The night before, she'd emptied out her own coffee-can savings—all the money she'd made from helping her mama out with seamstress jobs.

"Then crab you shall have!" Charlotte shouted.

"We have to drive a hard bargain, though, Lottie. Daddy says that's the most important thing to remember at the market."

"What's a bargain?" Charlotte asked.

Tiana laughed, hoisting up her basket. "Come on." But as they took another step into the market, they realized Big Daddy's path was taking a sharp left—toward a stall selling fresh beignets.

Oil sizzled in a giant pot over an open fire behind the stall. From the pot, the beignet maker removed hot lumps of fried dough with a pair of tongs. He tossed the beignets onto a big platter, coated them with powdered sugar, and laid them out for display. Tiana couldn't blame Big Daddy for following the smell—it was enough to make anyone's mouth water. She could never eat just one when she made them with her dad. But beignets were not what she had come to the market for.

"Big Daddy!" Charlotte had noticed her father's distraction as well.

"Oh, uh . . ." Big Daddy looked at the girls, then back at the tray. "I just need to, eh, do some business over here for a moment.

Make sure this sugar tastes okay. Go ahead with your shopping. Stay in this aisle and I'll catch up to you." Big Daddy turned back to the beignets and started grabbing them by the handful.

"Let's see what's up this way," Charlotte said, pulling Tiana deeper into the market.

They passed stalls selling all sorts of things Tiana had never seen before: exotic-looking fruits, smelly cheeses, unusual spices. One stall was even selling *frogs' legs,* of all things.

"Gross!" Tiana said as they walked by.

"Frogs' legs are a delicacy. Don't you know that?" Charlotte asked.

Tiana shook her head. "Uh-uh, Lottie. I don't like frogs alive, and I *certainly* don't like them . . . not alive."

They soon had everything Tiana needed. She found butter and flour, making an excellent deal on both. She found vegetables and spices at a reasonable price. She even found a lovely link of smoked pork sausage, which she got for a steal by pretending to walk away until the vendor lowered the cost. She bought a small bottle of hot sauce from a woman who made it from a family recipe. When she heard that Tiana was making gumbo for her daddy, the kind woman sold it to her for half price.

Finally, Tiana and Charlotte reached the stall selling the last ingredient on Tiana's list. She'd done so well at stretching every penny and charming the vendors that she had enough money left for at least one crab leg . . . maybe two.

"Last ingredient, Tiana," Charlotte said as they admired the display of fresh crab.

Tiana pictured her daddy's face glowing with happiness just as it had in her dream. "It's going to be the *best* gumbo ever."

She was just about to call the crab vendor over when she heard someone say "Pssst" behind her. "You want to make the best gumbo ever?" the voice said. "That won't make it the best. But I have something that will."

Tiana and Charlotte spun on their heels to see who was speaking to them. There stood a boy no older than they were. He was wearing a shirt and slacks that were nicer than anything anyone else was wearing in the market, except perhaps Big Daddy.

A worn gray beret sat atop his head.

Tiana frowned at him. "I know exactly how to make the best gumbo ever. And what I need to do it."

The boy shrugged, turning away. "If you say so," he said, strolling toward a stall at the end of the aisle. There were no products on display that Tiana could see from where she was standing. The only thing that stood out about the stall were the beads wrapped around the wooden posts.

Charlotte gripped Tiana's shoulders. "He's so handsome, don't you think?"

"Handsome?" Tiana made a face. "What does handsome have to do with anything?"

"Princes in fairy tales are always handsome," Charlotte said with a dreamy expression on her face. She glanced in the direction of the stall the boy had disappeared into.

Tiana snorted. "A prince? In the French Market? A fairy tale? Ha!"

"What?" Charlotte cried. "I've seen him at the market before. Maybe he's not a prince, but he could be someone special." She batted her eyelashes at Tiana. "What's the harm in taking a look at what he's selling?"

Tiana let out a sigh. Charlotte had been

helping her all day. She supposed she could return the favor. "Okay. We'll take a look—quickly!" she warned.

That was all it took to set Charlotte skipping off toward the mysterious stall. Tiana looked longingly at the crab legs before following her.

Chapter 5
A Magic Ingredient

Tiana stepped into the stall. Charlotte was running her fingers over the multicolored beads decorating the posts. It was completely empty inside except for a bookcase filled with bottles of strange-looking sauces. The boy was standing next to the case, waiting.

"*This* is what's going to make my gumbo the best ever?" Tiana asked the boy doubtfully. He just smirked and nodded toward the bottles.

She picked up one of the bottles to examine the liquid inside. It looked like green sauce. She shook the bottle gently. It sloshed around like . . . green sauce. She opened the cap and smelled it. It smelled like nothing. She returned the bottle to the shelf.

"That doesn't look like any gumbo ingredient I've ever seen," Tiana said, folding her arms.

The boy smirked again. "That's because it's not a gumbo ingredient. It's a *magic* ingredient."

"Magic?" Tiana frowned.

"Magic?!" That got Charlotte's attention. She darted away from the beads and grabbed one of the bottles.

"Magic sauce," the boy added.

"I already have hot sauce," Tiana said.

The boy shook his head. "Not hot.

Not cold. Not sweet. Not mild. *Magic.*
Guaranteed to make anything you add it to
taste the *best* it can possibly taste."

The boy's words had a smoothness to
them, almost as if he were singing. His
description came just a little too easily and a
little too quickly. But the word *best* stuck in
Tiana's ear.

"Oh, Tiana," Charlotte said, turning
the bottle over in her hands. "A magic
ingredient? You have to buy it. You have to!
Have to! Have to!"

Tiana tried to keep her head straight.
She'd set out to the market with a plan and a

list of ingredients. She'd known exactly what she was doing, and now . . . "I still have to buy crab. I don't have money for anything extra."

The boy chuckled. "With this magic sauce, you won't need crab. Your gumbo will taste like there's crab inside. In fact"— he smiled at Charlotte and she blushed—"it will taste like the whole ocean. Like there's shrimp, fish, crab, even *lobster* in that gumbo of yours."

"Lobster!" Charlotte cried.

Tiana shook her head. "One ingredient does all that? Sounds a lot like a shortcut. Taking the easy way. And that's not the way to make gumbo. That's not the way to do anything. At least, it's not the way my mama and daddy taught me."

The boy met Tiana's eyes. "Isn't the easy way doing what you already know?"

Tiana had never thought about it like that. "Well, I ought to at least *taste* this magic sauce."

"You can taste it," the boy said. "But if you taste it now, the magic will be gone by the time you put it in your gumbo."

"Gone? What kind of nonsense is that?" Tiana asked.

The boy shrugged. "That's just the way it works. It uses up its magic on whatever you

add it to. You want to waste that on a taste now, go ahead. But you taste it, you buy it."

Tiana cocked her head, thinking. The boy continued. "You can't really make the *best* gumbo ever if it isn't any different from what you've made before."

Best. There was that word again. It tugged at the dream still playing in her mind. She had pictured herself making gumbo the way she knew how, just like her daddy did. But the boy was right. How could it be the best if it was the same as it always was? Her dad deserved the *best.*

And then Tiana noticed something about the bottle in Charlotte's hands. A ray of sunlight bounced off the glass, and the green sauce sparkled in the light.

The gumbo in her dream had sparkled, too.

Tiana pulled her last coins from her purse and handed them to the boy. He nodded at her. Charlotte handed Tiana the bottle, beaming at her decision.

They left the stall and headed back down the aisle. Big Daddy was up ahead. It looked as if he'd moved on to sampling the sugar at the pie stand. Tiana tucked the bottle of magic sauce in her basket, hoping she was one step closer to the gumbo she'd seen in her dream.

Chapter 6
Chop, Mix, Stir

Whoosh. The stove fire blazed to life under the large pot.

"Thank you, Miss Emily," Tiana said to the cook. Big Daddy had insisted that Emily, the LaBouff family cook, start the fire on the stove and stay close by while the girls were in the kitchen.

"You sure you don't want help, Tiana?"

Miss Emily asked, eyeing Tiana's overflowing market basket.

"No, thank you. I'm going to make this gumbo myself from beginning to end," Tiana said with confidence.

"She won't even let *me* help, Miss Emily." Charlotte pouted.

"You girls just holler if you need anything." Miss Emily left the kitchen and Charlotte sat down on the floor to play with her pets.

Tiana was ready to begin. She looked at all the ingredients before her and got that happy stomach flip she always did before

cooking. She hopped onto the chair Miss Emily had set out so she could reach the stove. It was time to make Daddy proud.

The first step in making gumbo was the roux. She couldn't ruin it—she had just enough ingredients for one try. Tiana unwrapped the butter from the paper and dropped it into the pot, watching it sizzle and sputter. She added the flour bit by bit, stirring hard as she went. *Never stop stirring,* her daddy's voice rang in her head. The paste darkened from white to the color of rich caramel. *If you keep stirring, the roux will brown up so thick and rich and nice, that gumbo won't stand a chance to be anything but the best thing you've ever tasted. Stir, stir, stir. Add more flour. Stir, stir, stir.* When the roux reached the color of milk chocolate, she knew it was ready.

Tiana turned her attention to the next stage: the holy trinity of veggies she'd already chopped under Miss Emily's supervision. Into the pot they went. Then it was the sausage's turn, soaking up that veggie flavor and adding its smoky taste. Next came the broth she'd been simmering in another pot with all the spices.

It was fun doing this all by herself. With each ingredient, the aroma in the kitchen grew, letting Tiana know that the flavor was building just right. It smelled so good that Stella wandered away from Charlotte and sat at the bottom of Tiana's stool, hoping to catch any drops that might fall. Tiana didn't blame her. She finally snuck a spoonful herself, and . . . *Mmmm!* If it didn't taste just as good as her daddy's gumbo! Not *quite* the best yet, though.

It was time to add the magic ingredient.

Tiana picked up the bottle. She saw the sparkle again as the light from the stove fire reflected off of it. "Here goes nothing," she

said as she poured a few drops of magic into the gumbo.

She stirred and watched, waiting. For what, she wasn't sure. Fireworks? Something magical to happen? She took a small sip. The gumbo tasted just the same.

Tiana added more sauce. Considering it was magic, she figured the more the better. As she stirred, she noticed that the mixture was thickening. Something *was* happening after all! She added more magic sauce. The gumbo was getting harder to stir. Nervous, Tiana added even more, hoping it would turn the stew into something *magical* soon . . . but her gumbo was quickly turning into something more like glue! The wooden spoon was sticking straight up from the pot, as if it were stuck in a vat of gooey swamp mud.

"Uh-oh," Tiana said. She scrambled off the stool and filled a pitcher with water, hoping she could thin the stew out. She raced back over to the stove and poured the water in, trying to get it back to the tasty soup it had been just moments before. But when Tiana added the water, something very strange happened. The gumbo started frothing, roiling, bubbling up, up, *up* the sides of the pot.

"Uh-oh!" Tiana yelled. Charlotte raced over just in time to see the top of the gumbo slosh over the sides of the pot and spill onto the floor.

"Uh-oh!" Charlotte echoed.

Tiana dove out of the way and hid behind the counter, Charlotte, Marcel, and Stella on her heels. They watched, wincing, as the stew continued to pour onto the floor like a gumbo volcano.

After what felt like forever, the pot finally stopped spitting out gumbo. Tiana approached the stove. She nudged at the remaining gumbo with the spoon. It wasn't gumbo anymore. It was some kind of dark sludge, thick and stiff. She wasn't sure she'd even be able to get the spoon out.

This was not the best gumbo ever. This was the *worst* gumbo ever. Tiana's dream vanished in front of her eyes.

Chapter 7
Not So Magic After All

Tiana slumped down on the floor and let her tears fall. Stella trotted over to her and licked the salty tears streaming down her cheeks. Charlotte knelt and placed a hand on her friend's shoulder.

"Do you want to start again?" she asked softly. "You were doing so well."

Tiana shook her head, tears flowing.

"I only had enough money for the ingredients I already bought. They're gone now. I ruined the gumbo."

"But we have some of those ingredients here. And Big Daddy could take us to buy the rest in the morning," Charlotte said.

Charlotte and Big Daddy were always generous with their good fortune. But it didn't feel right to take from their pantries. *Everything* felt wrong now. Tiana wouldn't be using the ingredients she'd earned. And even though the magic sauce was silly and clearly not magic at all, she couldn't shake the feeling the boy had put in her head. The same gumbo she'd always made with her daddy wasn't going to be any different. It wasn't going to be the *best*.

"I failed, Lottie. Maybe I wasn't meant to make the best gumbo ever. Maybe the dream I had was just that . . . a dream, meant to stay in my head at night and not come into the day." Tiana sniffled.

"I was sure magic was going to be the key," Charlotte said as she sat down next to Tiana.

"I tried to take the easy way . . . and that was wrong." Tiana scratched Stella's ear, thanking her for drying her tears. "I'd better get to cleaning. This mess isn't pretty." Tiana

fetched a rag and bucket from the broom
closet.

"I'll help," Charlotte said.

"You're going to clean?" Tiana asked,
surprised.

"Oh—I meant I was going to ask Miss
Emily or the maid to come in and do it."
Charlotte looked at the cleaning supplies
in Tiana's hands, realizing that her friend

had something different in mind. "But you're right. No more easy way tonight!"

Charlotte grabbed a rag and, after studying the way Tiana scrubbed the floor with soap and water, began to help. The girls wiped up the gumbo sludge from the stove, the floor, and the pot. When the LaBouffs' kitchen was finally back to normal, over an hour had passed, and the girls were exhausted. Charlotte took the rag out of Tiana's hands and led her upstairs, a friendly hand on her shoulder.

A short while later, Tiana was tucked into a cot between Charlotte's bed and the big window that looked out onto the starry sky.

Charlotte's whisper broke the silence. "How about that evening star, Tiana?" she said. "Wish on it. Wish, wish, wish, and things will work out tomorrow."

Tiana sighed. "If only a wish were enough, Lottie. That star can't make gumbo better than I can." She paused. "Well, actually . . . maybe it can."

Charlotte sighed in return, and Tiana heard her nestle deeper under her covers. "Good night, Tiana."

"Good night, Lottie." But Tiana kept her eyes fixed on the evening star. It almost seemed to wink at her, begging her to try her luck on a silly magical thing for the second time that day. *Okay, Star,* Tiana thought. *If there's any magic in the world—even just a sparkle—maybe you could find a way to send some of it to me tomorrow.*

And then she closed her eyes and slipped into a dreamless sleep.

Chapter 8
Facing the Neighborhood

The next morning, Tiana woke still feeling glum. At breakfast, even Charlotte's most enthusiastic attempts to cheer her up didn't help. As Big Daddy drove her home, Tiana told the LaBouffs she'd decided to cancel the party.

"Cancel?" Charlotte placed her palms on her cheeks in shock. "But you can still have a party, gumbo or no gumbo."

Tiana shook her head, miserable. "I promised everyone they would taste the *best* gumbo ever. And now I have nothing. I can't embarrass Daddy like that."

Big Daddy cleared his throat. "Tiana, there's nothing you could ever do that would embarrass your dad. He loves you more than he loves gumbo, more than he loves New Orleans, more than he loves anything. You can try your darnedest, but you can't disappoint him."

Although Tiana heard his words, they didn't land in her heart. "Thank you, Big Daddy and Charlotte, for your hospitality and your help in taking me to the market.

But it's better that you don't come tonight."

Charlotte frowned. When the car stopped in front of Tiana's house, Big Daddy got out to open her door. "You send word, and I'll have New Orleans's finest chefs over here in no time to make your dad a five-star meal. Remember: you always make your dad proud. And you make Charlotte and me proud, too."

Tiana turned her head quickly so Big Daddy wouldn't see the fresh tears springing up in her eyes. "Good-bye!" she called. The car chugged away down the street and out of sight.

Tiana wiped away her tears and trudged

into her kitchen. Her mama was at the table, sewing. She looked up in surprise. "You're home earlier than I expected. Are Charlotte and Big Daddy coming in with the gumbo?"

Tiana sat down next to her mama, studying the ribbon in her hands. Perhaps if she looked interested enough in the ribbon, her mama wouldn't notice —

"What happened? I know that face," her mama said in no time at all.

Tiana took a deep breath and told her the whole story, from the beignets, to the bargaining, to the magic sauce, to the gumbo sludge. Her mama listened, staying quiet until the story was over. "Tiana, we can go out right now and get more ingredients. I'll help you. There's still time."

Tiana shook her head. Something didn't feel right. She felt as if she'd never find the gumbo from her dream, as if everything had been turned upside down. "It's no use, Mama."

"No use? Is that what we've taught you, Tiana? That it's no use when something goes a little wrong to try again?" her mama asked sternly.

"No," Tiana grumbled.

"Plus, it's your daddy's birthday. He

doesn't know what you're planning, but he knows something secret is going on. We don't want to let him down, do we?"

"Mama, I feel bad enough. I know all that. . . ." Tiana turned her eyes back to the ribbon and its pretty blue sheen. Her mama didn't need magic ingredients for her dresses. Her hands and her talent made magic from ordinary things. "I know," she whispered.

Her mama picked up her sewing needle and got back to stitching. "Well, the people on this block are expecting a party. So you'll have to go and explain that there won't be any gumbo tonight."

Tiana cringed. "Do I have to?"

Tiana's mama gave her a look that said yes.

Outside, Tiana faced the first house: the new neighbor. It would be the most difficult house, the one with the person inside who didn't know her at all. Better to start with the hardest first.

Tiana gathered her strength and marched up to the front door to knock. It took a long minute, but Mrs. Marquez finally answered. Tiana opened her mouth to explain why she was there, but the smell of smoke rising in the air made her pause. "Is something burning?"

Mrs. Marquez's eyes widened in alarm, and she raced back inside. Tiana wasn't sure whether she should follow her without invitation, but her concern won out.

Once in the kitchen, Tiana found Mrs. Marquez leaning over charred lumps on the stove. Mrs. Marquez shrugged at Tiana. "They were supposed to be beignets."

Tiana didn't know what to say. She had never seen a beignet, not even a ruined one, look like the black mess on the stove.

Mrs. Marquez shook her head. "*Ay.* I know. I tasted one last week when I was exploring your city. So delicious, so light, it was like biting into a cloud." Mrs. Marquez threw the ruined beignets into the wastebasket. "These are more like rocks."

She sat down at the table, motioning

for Tiana to join her. "I was a good baker at home. But these beignets are giving me so much trouble!" Something in Mrs. Marquez's expression matched the feeling in Tiana's heart. Not getting it right. Failing.

But then Tiana brightened. "My daddy and I make beignets all the time. I can help you!"

Mrs. Marquez smiled. "I wanted to make a perfect batch to bring to your party."

Tiana's face fell. The party. In the delight of being able to solve one problem, she'd forgotten about her own—just for the moment.

"*Que pasa,* Tiana?" Mrs. Marquez asked. "I can see on your face . . . something is not right."

Tiana felt the tears come back. Mrs. Marquez reached out and placed her hand over Tiana's. "Tell me about it."

Chapter 9
Sharing Dreams

When Tiana finished speaking, the tears weren't quite done.

"Cry all you need to. Let it out," Mrs. Marquez soothed.

Tiana wiped her eyes.

"What is your father like?" Mrs. Marquez asked.

Tiana didn't know where to start. "He loves my mama. He loves me. He loves food and cooking. We're going to have a restaurant someday. Tiana's Place."

Mrs. Marquez nodded. "He sounds like a very good father. Does he give you advice?"

Tiana grinned. "He's always giving advice. 'Work hard, Tiana.' 'Dream big, Tiana.' 'Don't take the easy way, Tiana. . . .'" Her voice trailed off. "But I did this time. Just this once, I thought maybe . . . maybe a shortcut would work. I thought it might be good to try something different. But I was wrong."

"Your father sounds very wise," Mrs. Marquez said with a smile. "And remember, never be afraid of being different or being wrong. How will you know what's right unless you make mistakes first?" She leaned forward in her chair. "I also know something about the easy way. And something about the hard way." Tiana looked up, surprised. Mrs. Marquez nodded. "In my life, the easy way was never an option. Much like what your dad says. Life is hard, dear Tiana. It will never

be easy. Not if you're doing it right. Not if you're chasing your dreams and following that evening star."

Tiana couldn't believe what she was hearing. This stranger from somewhere far away . . . she was saying the same things her daddy always said. "Is that what you did? Chase your dreams here?"

Mrs. Marquez smiled, but it was a sad smile. "Not just my dream. It was always a dream of my husband's that one day we'd end up here together. But I lost him last year. And suddenly, nothing seemed more important than getting here. Making at least part of our dream come true."

"I'm sorry about your husband," Tiana said.

"Chasing dreams can be difficult work," Mrs. Marquez continued. "Getting to this city, to this country, all the way from Cuba . . . that was nowhere near easy." She shook her head. "But it's important work." She pointed at Tiana. "And I think important work is something both you and your daddy understand well."

Tiana's heart lifted. Telling her story, having a good cry, listening to Mrs. Marquez, thinking of her daddy . . . it was making everything feel a little lighter.

"Now, enough serious talk. How about

some lunch?" Mrs. Marquez asked. "Crying can make a person very hungry. My soup is almost ready."

Tiana looked at the stove. With the smoky smell almost gone, she detected a spicy, hearty fragrance coming from a pot on the stovetop. It smelled delicious!

"Would you like to taste?" Mrs. Marquez asked, offering Tiana a spoon. "Sofrito: Spanish onions, garlic, bell peppers, tomato sauce, and a few other special spices. Just about ready to go in the broth. I make it every day. It tastes like home, and all I miss there."

Tiana bolted up out of her chair, eager to taste. "I know what you mean," she said, reaching for the spoon. "My daddy always says food brings people together. People from all walks of life."

Tiana took a bite of the sofrito. As the flavors hit her tongue, she was struck with an idea. There *was* a way to save her daddy's party after all!

Chapter 10
The New Plan

Tiana had a new plan. A *different* plan. But this time, it felt like the right kind of different.

"Mrs. Marquez," she said, "instead of turning this sofrito into stew, could you lend it to me?" Tiana's eye caught the sack on the counter, overflowing with white powder. "And maybe some of that flour? I could really use it for the party."

Mrs. Marquez beamed. "But what will we eat for lunch?"

"My mama can make us sandwiches. She's really good at that!" Tiana said.

"I'll tell you what," Mrs. Marquez said. "I'll let you use my kitchen so you can keep the gumbo a secret if you show me what I'm doing wrong with these beignets."

Tiana grinned. "It's a deal!" She shook Mrs. Marquez's hand and explained her new plan. She was flooded with inspiration— maybe that evening star did have a little magic in it.

She ran across the street to her house, swinging her front door open and shouting,

"Mama!" But for the second time in a few short days, the sight of her daddy in the kitchen took her by surprise. She hadn't expected him home for hours.

"Daddy!" she exclaimed. Her father was sitting at the kitchen table, reading the newspaper and drinking coffee.

"Well, don't look so disappointed to see me, baby!" Tiana's dad held out his arms for her. Tiana ran to him. She looked over his shoulder at her mama, who was standing in the kitchen doorway.

"Happy birthday, Daddy! I didn't expect you home so soon," she said.

"I asked the boss to let me off early. On

account of wanting to spend my special day with my two favorite girls," he said.

Tiana pulled out of his hug. "Mama, can I speak to you for a moment in private?" Tiana tried to pretend this was a request she made every day as she dragged her mama into her bedroom.

"Is that secret plan bubbling back up again?" her mama asked.

"I don't have time to explain, Mama. The party is back on. You'll just have to trust me," Tiana said.

"Oh?" Her mama folded her arms and gave Tiana a look.

"Yes! Mama, I'm trying to make a dream come true. For Daddy."

Her mama considered this and finally nodded. "What do you need from me?"

"I need two sandwiches. And I need you to distract Daddy so he doesn't see me taking his gumbo pot." Tiana knew she was asking for a lot. But it had to work.

Her mama laughed. "I'll send him on an errand. And where might you be taking these sandwiches and your dad's precious pot?"

"To Mrs. Marquez's house."

Her mama raised her eyebrows.

"To make a dream come true, Mama," Tiana repeated.

"Give me two minutes." Tiana's mom winked and headed for the door.

"Make sure he's dressed up in his good suit by five p.m., too!" Tiana whispered. Then she sat on her bed and counted every second up to one hundred and twenty. Finally, she tiptoed back out into the kitchen. Her daddy was gone, and her mama was at the counter slicing bread.

It took a few moments and some wrestling, but Tiana got the gumbo pot out of the cupboard. Her mama held out two sandwiches, wrapped tight in paper. "Just put them in the pot," Tiana said. Her mama did as she asked. "Thank you!" Tiana called as she ran out the door.

Tiana needed to talk to every neighbor who was coming to the party—and fast. First stop was Grandma Marnie's. Grandma was in her usual spot in her rocking chair on the porch. "Grandma Marnie," Tiana called as she ran up the porch steps, hugging the gumbo pot. "I need a little help."

"Lucky for you, help is my specialty," Grandma Marnie said with a wink.

"I'm missing a few—well, most of my gumbo ingredients. Do you have something you can contribute? I'm making the *best* gumbo ever. Don't forget." Tiana smiled her best smile.

"A chance to contribute to the *best* gumbo ever?" Grandma Marnie said. "I'd be honored. Let me see what I've got inside."

Grandma Marnie disappeared into her house. Moments later she returned with a sack, holding it open for Tiana to see. Inside was a pile of . . . "Are those chicken bones?" Tiana asked.

"Sure are," Grandma Marnie said. "The

best soup bones you can find. I was saving them for a midweek stew, but I have a feeling they were meant to be in your gumbo."

"Thanks!" Tiana said, and she gratefully accepted the bag of bones. She moved the sandwiches and tossed the bones into the pot. Then she waved good-bye to Grandma Marnie.

Next up was the Monroe house. Tiana knocked on the door, hoping Emile wouldn't answer. But of course he did. As soon as he saw Tiana, he closed the door until she could only see a sliver of his eye.

Tiana kneeled. "Emile, I'm your friend.

Tiana, from across the way." She spoke in the sweetest voice possible. "I need a little help. Do you think you could help me?"

To her surprise, Emile nodded.

"Wonderful!" Tiana said. "Could you fetch your mama? I need some gumbo ingredients."

Emile's eye disappeared. A few moments later the door opened wider, and Annette Monroe appeared.

"Tiana," Annette said. "Will these work?" She dropped several bay leaves into the gumbo pot.

"Thank you!" Tiana said.

"Looking forward to seeing you later," Annette said.

Tiana moved down the rest of the block. Instead of telling the neighbors the party was canceled, she asked for one gumbo ingredient from each household. From the Dupres, she received a pouch of fresh sea salt. From the Potters, a handful of several divine-smelling spices. From the Keans, a large pat of freshly churned butter. From the Gilmores, the butchers, she got a handful of fresh sausage links. The Rices, to Tiana's great surprise, handed her a bag of white rice. And finally, the Wildes gave her a pail full of fresh water. Mr. Wilde even helped her carry it back to Mrs. Marquez's.

As she walked through Mrs. Marquez's door, Tiana felt a surge of confidence. Yesterday she thought she had magic on her side, but today she felt armed with a different kind of magic. She had magic ingredients from the people around her. The people who always made her daddy's gumbo taste even better just by being there to share the meal.

When she reached the kitchen, Mrs. Marquez had the sofrito sizzling and ready. Tiana placed the gumbo pot on the kitchen table. As they ate their sandwiches, Tiana organized all her ingredients. Then she headed to the stove with her trusty pot and began the roux. Nothing—not the memory of yesterday's ruined gumbo or the pressure of making her daddy's night perfect—was going to let her fail now.

She added the pat of butter from the

Keans and stirred in Mrs. Marquez's flour. Slowly, surely, the roux turned the perfect shade of chocolate brown. In another pot, Tiana boiled Grandma Marnie's chicken bones in the Wildes' water with the Dupres' salt. The Gilmores' sausage went sizzling into the roux along with Mrs. Marquez's sofrito: a Cuban take on the holy vegetable trinity. Once the broth was boiling and the roux/sofrito/sausage mixture was ready, Tiana combined everything with the Monroes' bay leaves and the mysterious spices from the Potters. With the rich stew simmering, Tiana set to work helping Mrs. Marquez with the beignets.

The dough had been made just right, Tiana explained as she helped Mrs. Marquez form it into small, flat squares. The problem was that the oil was so hot, the beignets burned as soon as she dropped them in. Tiana showed Mrs. Marquez how to test the oil temperature by tearing off a tiny lump of dough and seeing how long it took to brown. They increased the fire little by little, until the lump turned gold not instantly, but within a minute. Once the oil was the right temperature, they plopped in their squares. To Mrs. Marquez's delight, the dough puffed and shimmered, turning a deep golden brown instead of charred black.

Together, they fried the beignets, coating them in powdered sugar after they came out of the oil.

Mrs. Marquez and Tiana helped themselves to one beignet each—just to make sure they were done right. Then they each had another for good measure.

After some time, Tiana tasted her own creation. The gumbo was just as good as it had been the day before, before she ruined it with the "magic" ingredient. The Rices' rice was cooked and ready for the rich brown stew to be ladled over the top. But something was still missing.

"Watch the stove, could you, Mrs.

Marquez?" Tiana asked. "I'll be right back!"

Tiana returned home. As she entered the kitchen, there her daddy was again.

"I know you're up to something, Tiana," he said behind her as she searched the cupboard. It had to be there. She couldn't not have her favorite ingredient. Not now.

There it was.

"Daddy, do you mind closing your eyes for a minute?" Tiana asked.

"Baby, as long as you aren't in any trouble, I'll close my eyes for a week." He laughed.

"I'll see you soon, Daddy!" Tiana cried, and ran back across the street. Mrs. Marquez was standing guard over the stove. Tiana looked at the bottle of hot sauce in her hands. Just enough left. She poured it into the mixture, stirred, and let it sit for a minute. She dipped the wooden spoon and tasted.

Perfect.

Chapter 11
The Feast

An hour later, Tiana was back at her house getting it ready for the party. Tiana's mama was distracting her daddy in the other room, fussing over his tie. After Tiana had swept the porch and cleared everything off the table, she swung the front door open wide, signaling to the neighborhood that the party was ready to begin.

Mrs. Marquez was the first to arrive. She

balanced a tray of beignets over the top of the gumbo pot. Tiana rushed to help her, setting the gumbo down on the stove and the beignets on the table.

Then came Grandma Marnie and the rest of the Johnson family. To Tiana's surprise, Grandma Marnie was carrying several plates of her famous corn bread. "It's no party without corn bread," she said, placing the plates on the table beside the beignets.

Next the Monroes arrived. Emile approached Tiana shyly, offering her a large bowl of potato salad. "Mama says potato salad goes with everything, Miss Tiana," he said, handing her the bowl and running back to Annette.

Then came the Gilmores with a platter of hush puppies. "Every New Orleans feast has to have hush puppies," Papa Gilmore said, hugging Tiana as he put the tray on the table.

The Potters brought a large pitcher of sweet tea. The Keans contributed a mound of mashed potatoes, and the Rices brought a platter of freshly shucked corn. As dish after dish piled up next to Mrs. Marquez's beignets, it seemed the gumbo party was turning into a feast fit for a king.

Just as Tiana was about to call for her parents, Big Daddy and Charlotte walked in the door. "But I told you the party was canceled!" Tiana cried out in surprise as Charlotte covered her in hugs and blond curls. In all the rush of re-planning the party, Tiana had completely forgotten to let them know it was back on!

"Now, Tiana," Big Daddy said with a smile. He was speaking to her, but his eyes were fixed on Mrs. Marquez's platter of beignets. "We knew better than to give up on you."

Charlotte whispered, "Plus, we came by a few hours ago to check, and your mama told us the party was happening after all." She looked around the kitchen. "I knew you could do it, Tiana. I'm sorry I distracted you with that silly magic stuff."

"I had a hand in that, too, Lottie. No one made me buy that sauce but me," Tiana said.

"It turned out for the best, though."

Charlotte held up a paper sack. "We brought something, too." She opened the bag to reveal a mound of crabs. She plucked one out and held it in the air.

"You didn't have to do that," Tiana said as she clasped the sack. "Thank you, Big Daddy."

Big Daddy grinned, his mouth covered in sugar.

Tiana emptied the bag into the still-simmering gumbo. "I think it's time," she whispered to the crowd gathered in her kitchen and spilling out onto the porch.

She crept down the hallway to her parents' bedroom.

"Daddy? Could you come out to the kitchen for a moment?" Tiana asked.

"You finally want to show me what you've been up to?" Her daddy reached a hand out to Tiana, and she took it in her own and led him to the kitchen.

"Surprise!" everyone shouted.

Her daddy laughed and laughed and laughed. Tiana wasn't sure whether he was surprised, but she *was* sure he was happy. "You did all this for me?" he asked.

"I wanted to make you the best party

ever. The best *gumbo* ever," Tiana said.

Her dad looked at the table. "Something's for sure—this is going to be the best meal I've ever eaten. I can tell just by looking." He squeezed Tiana's hand. "Where's this gumbo I'm smelling?"

This was it—the moment Tiana had seen in her dream. She was surrounded by all the neighborhood families—Big Daddy, Charlotte, her new friend Mrs. Marquez, her mama, and especially her daddy. It was better than her dream. It was real.

"Have a taste, Daddy," Tiana said, handing him a spoon.

"Did you make this all by yourself?" he asked.

"I made it—but I had help," Tiana said. "From everyone here. Even you."

Her daddy dipped the spoon into the gumbo pot and lifted it to his mouth. He tasted, swallowed, and smacked his lips.

"Mmmm-*mm,* Tiana," he said. "That is, without a doubt, the *best* gumbo ever."

Tiana wrapped her arms around her daddy in a giant hug. He'd said the words she'd been longing to hear. As she held him tight, something about the gumbo caught her eye.

She was sure it had sparkled.